Emerald Cove

The Tale of Dougie Woodbridge

By Si Baker

CONTENTS PAGE

Chapter One: Bacon Bear.

The index finger of a man named Dougie Woodbridge presses a button on a home coffee machine, and an orange light illuminates. The finger moves away as steam rises from a waffle machine, and piping-hot sounds crackle away, signalling that the waffles are cooking nicely.

Dougie's hand tugs at the front handle of the waffle machine. On the second attempt, he manages to pull the handle up, and steam gushes out. After the initial burst of steam, the breakfast waffles become visible inside. His hand moves to grab a black spatula, and once he has it, he approaches the waffles. The waffles are flipped over one by one, hastily, not by someone you would consider a chef. After checking for brownness, Dougie moves towards two red tartan-patterned dinner plates.

These plates rest on a brown wooden kitchen worktop. He picks up the first plate with his left hand and takes it to the waffle machine. The spatula grabs a waffle from the front left of the machine and places it on top of another waffle to its right.

Once Dougie finishes plating up, he carries them to a table in an open kitchen. The table is covered with a white tablecloth, though some of the dark wood underneath is still visible, especially at the corners. The table is set for two people, with two red polka dot table mats and white side plates to the left of them. Four dark wooden chairs surround the table.

The table is adorned with various items: a carton of milk, two types of juice (one orange, one lemon, both in tall patterned glass jars), two red empty bowls stacked on each other, two empty mugs (green and yellow), and two small glasses for juice. An open pot of sugar (black wooden) with a silver stainless steel teaspoon inside.

A white plate displays four croissants and four blueberry muffins. Four clear plastic cereal containers hold cornflakes, Fruit Loops, choco-cereal, and Lucky Stars. An assortment of jams, a half-filled plastic bottle (with a red label) of maple syrup, and a quarter-filled jar of Sunpat (peanut butter). A white dinner plate boasts streaky bacon, and there is some toast on a separate plate.

Additionally, stainless steel cutlery is piled up (forks, butter knives, teaspoons, and tablespoons) in no particular order, ready to be used when needed.

Dougie walks across the room, placing the plates one by one onto the table mats. Dougie himself has black, shoe-polished hair, and he wears a white fitted shirt tucked into his black fitted trousers. His outfit is completed with a black leather belt featuring a classy, thin silver buckle, and his black leather shoes have been heavily polished. He exudes confidence.

He pulls out a wooden chair, which has a black fitted blazer resting on the back of the seat, and then takes a seat. He picks up a glass with his right hand, pulls it towards him, and grabs a jar of orange juice with his left hand, pouring it into the glass. After finishing, he puts the jar back and pushes his glass to the side.

Using both hands, he picks up a blueberry muffin and a croissant, placing them on a side plate, separate from the waffle plate. From the cutlery pile, he selects a butter knife and opens a jar of strawberry and blueberry jam.

Steadily holding the croissant with his left hand, he uses his right hand to cut it open and fill it with jam.

A black fluffy German Shepherd named Bear, with blonde paws and ears and a long tongue, enters the room and approaches Dougie. Dougie smiles and embraces his dog, giving it strokes and hugs. A thirteen-year-old girl named Ariel, with shoulder-length blonde hair, enters the room shortly after Bear. Ariel is dressed in a fresh new school uniform.

Ariel stops just in front of the doorway and strikes a fashionable pose for her father, Dougie, who looks up at her while still stroking his dog. "Look at you, very posh. Are you ready for your first day?"

Ariel smiles, stops posing, and walks over to the coffee pot. "About as ready as I can be. How about you? Are you looking forward to your first day at work?"

"About as ready as I can be. The coffee should be ready if you want some."

"Ace." Ariel heads to the coffee pot and loosens it, while Dougie picks up some maple syrup and pours it over his waffles.

There's an old-looking blue retro radio in the room, though it's actually a new digital radio. Ariel picks up the fresh coffee pot and turns on the radio, which plays some relaxing jazz funk. Ariel walks over to the table, rearranging the jams to make space for the coffee pot, and then sets it down.

Ariel grabs a piece of bacon and tosses it on the floor for the dog, which eagerly devours it as she takes a seat. She picks up the choco-cereal container, opens the flap, and pours the cereal into the bowl. Ariel then picks up the carton of milk, while Dougie watches her, a small amount of pastry flakes in his mouth. They quietly eat their breakfast without speaking, content in each other's company. Dougie picks up the coffee pot and pours himself a coffee into his mug, then sets the coffee pot down. Steam rises from the mug.

Ariel picks up another piece of bacon and tosses it to the dog, then takes two more pieces and places them on her waffles before continuing to eat her cereal.

Dougie takes a sip of his coffee, his face lighting up as he swallows. "Aaah, that's a good mug of coffee."

He looks at his gold watch and then at the clock on the wall; both show the time as 8:08 AM. He glances at his watch again as Ariel looks at him, her spoon near her mouth, about to take the next bite, but she pauses and smirks.

"Late again?" Ariel wonders as she puts a spoonful of cereal in her mouth.

Dougie stands up and nods in agreement. He picks up the suit blazer hanging from the back of

the chair and then walks around the table
towards his daughter. Just as she's about to
take another spoonful of cereal, he puts his arm
around the back of her head and gives her a kiss
on the cheek, her mouth full. "Have a great first
day at school. Try and make some friends if you
can."

Ariel rolls her eyes and gives him a sarcastic
smile as Dougie gives Bear a big stroke on the
head.

"Okay, maybe that could be a long shot. Are you
going to be okay walking to school?"

"Dad, stop worrying. This isn't the first time
I've had to go to a new school. And this town is
so small compared to New York; it's not like I
need a map to get there."

"Okay, you know I worry."

Ariel looks at him lovingly and notices that his black tie is loose. She waves him over to come closer. "Dad, come here."

He walks over, smiling but slightly curious as to why his daughter is standing up from her seat. She puts her arms on him, one on each of his arms, pauses for a moment, takes her arms off, and then moves them towards his tie. She starts pulling up his tie to the top button and smartens it up. She quickly gives him a peck on the cheek when she's done.

"Thank you. Right, I best be going. Have a good day."

"See ya later, Dad. Love you." Ariel returns to her seat, picks up her bowl of cereal, and starts eating.

Dougie starts walking towards the doorway, giving his dog another pat on the head. By the doorway, there's a leather briefcase, and he starts walking past it as he looks back at his daughter.

"Love you too," Dougie said as he headed out the door.

Ariel then glanced down at the briefcase and shouted quickly yet calmly, "Dad!" before returning to eating her cereal.

Dougie poked his head around the dark wooden-framed doorway and looked at his daughter. "Yes, darling?"

Ariel nodded slightly, gesturing toward Dougie's briefcase. "Your briefcase."

Dougie shifted his focus from his daughter to the side, where he noticed his briefcase. He paused briefly before placing his hand on it. Dougie lowered his arm and then picked up the briefcase again, looking back at his daughter.

"Thank you, love you." He hurried out of the doorway.

Meanwhile, Ariel shook her head, poured herself a coffee, and took a sip. "Aaah, that's some good coffee."

Chapter Two: Pen.

Morag sat behind a desk at Emerald Cove police station, surrounded by blue walls with wood accents. She was on the phone, using a headset at her computer desk. Morag wore pink-rimmed glasses, had blonde permed hair, bright pink lipstick, and a pink fluffy woolly jumper.

Behind her was a green door leading to the room, bearing a silver nameplate with "Morag Monrel" in capital letters. Morag had a high-pitched yet professional receptionist's voice.

The reception/help desk featured a wooden counter with security glass across the front, and a portion was open for communication. A glass pane that would usually be there had been slid aside to facilitate conversation with the receptionist.

On the desk, there was a money plant, the back of a photo frame, and a digital clock. To the left of the door (behind Morag), there was another countertop with a fax machine, a printer, and a large calculator. The wall behind Morag was composed of rich brown wood slabs, and a poster/picture of Van Gogh's "Sunflowers" adorned the wall.

Morag was deeply engrossed in her conversation, while Dougie entered the reception room, dressed smartly and holding his briefcase. He approached the desk, gave Morag a polite wave with his free hand, but she didn't notice or respond to him. Dougie lowered his arm, patiently waiting and listening to her conversation while scanning his surroundings briefly. Eventually, he looked back at Morag.

Morag kept Dougie waiting as she continued her conversation. "Well, can't you put it around the back like the note said?" A prolonged silence followed as she awaited a reply, curling a bit of her fringe around a pen.

"Well, when I brought it, I put a note saying I won't be there to sign for it. So can you put it around the back in the shed? And in case of an emergency, I gave you my work number."

Dougie overheard the silence while she waited for a reply. "Well, I can't sign it if I'm not there." Morag then looked up at Dougie, doing a little surprised jump in her chair as she noticed the man standing there, smiling at her. She put her hand on her heart to calm herself down.

She looked at Dougie, took her hand off her heart, and raised her index finger (as a form of body language) while mouthing that she'd be with him in a minute. Morag then looked back down at her desk to concentrate on the

conversation. "That's why I couldn't pick it up or
be there."

Another pause in silence continued as Morag
listened to the reply, and then she looked at the
man waiting. They both smiled at each other as
if it were the first time. Morag then moved the
mouse on the computer and looked at the screen.
"At Emerald Cove police station."

Again, another pause in silence followed. Morag
looked at Dougie, and they exchanged smiles
once more, as if meeting for the first time.
Morag then pointed over to the ready-made
coffee pot.

Dougie glanced over and then back at Morag,
thanking her with a thumbs-up hand signal and
holding it for a little longer than necessary.

Morag smiled, and Dougie walked over to the
table with the coffee. He placed his briefcase on
the bottom base so it stood upright in a

handle-grabbing position. "Well, that's what the note said, and I never had a follow-up message to say it would be a problem."

The coffee pot sat on an average-sized dark wooden coffee table to the left, near the wall connecting to the corridor. The table had a white and red checked cloth on top, and its contents included seven mugs of different colours, a jug of milk, a glass pot of brown and white sugar, a hot pot of water on a hot plate, and a wooden wicker basket with patterned kitchen roll pressed in along with loose tea bags.

Dougie picked up a yellow mug with his left hand and then used his right hand to pour himself a black coffee from the coffee pot. Morag continued her conversation, "No, you misunderstand me."

After pouring his coffee, Dougie placed the pot back where it was. He didn't add any sugar or milk to his coffee. Once he had his coffee, he picked up his briefcase by the handle with his right hand and walked over to Morag.

"No, I work here. Okay, thank you. See you shortly," Morag hangs up. Dougie looks over at Morag with his yellow coffee cup and takes a sip. Morag gazes at Dougie and gives him a smile. "Hello, sir. Sorry for keeping you waiting. How may I help you today?"

Dougie walks closer to Morag and smiles. "Hello, Detective Dougie Woodbridge."

Morag's smile changes, and she adopts a more concentrated expression. "Sorry, Detective Dougie Woodbridge is not here. He doesn't start his first day until later this morning."

Dougie maintains his smile. "No, I am Detective Dougie Woodbridge."

"No, like I said, he's not in until later today. I can leave a message and say you stopped by.

What's your name?" Morag grabbed a black pen from her desk; the other one was tangled in her hair. She brought the notepad closer for comfortable writing.

Dougie leaned closer to the counter. "My name is Detective Dougie Woodbridge."

Morag continued writing and then looked up at him, pausing. She looked at the name and then at him as Dougie smiled. "Your name is Detective Dougie Woodbridge?"

"That's correct."

"So you don't want me to leave this message?"

"That's correct."

Morag stood up, extended her right hand for a handshake, the pen embedded in her hair. Dougie extended his right hand for a handshake and smiled. "My name is Morag. So you're here for your first day?"

"That's correct. I believe I need to meet Sheriff Steve Hughes?"

They stopped shaking hands, and Morag looked at him, processing his words. She then replied while pointing at the green door, "No problem, I'll take you to Sheriff Steve Hughes's office. Just hang on for a second, and I'll come around through this green door."

Morag took off her headset and placed it on the desk. She turned around and opened the green door, walking through it. Dougie stood there, sipping his yellow mug of coffee.

Morag reappeared from around the corner into the corridor and met Dougie. They stood in front of each other, looking at each other for a bit longer than necessary, as if they had forgotten why she had come around the corner.

Dougie pointed vaguely, "Sheriff Steve Hughes?"

Morag gave a look as if she remembered why she came around and then pointed to the right, starting to walk that way and waving for him to follow. "Sheriff Steve Hughes' office is this way. Come with me, and I'll show you."

Dougie smiled and began walking down the corridor, taking more large sips of coffee along the way. They stopped at a red door with a plaque that said 'Sheriff Steve Hughes.'

Morag opened the door, revealing Sheriff Steve Hughes, who was sitting behind his desk. He had white-grey hair under his sheriff hat and sat in a green leather chair with wooden arms. His wooden desk had a large square patch of red in the middle, where a computer and a pen holder filled with pens, pencils, a ruler, and a rubber were placed. Stacks of paper and various documents cluttered the desk. A black leather diary, sports trophies, and an old-school blackboard on a wooden stand also adorned the room.

Behind the sheriff was a bookcase filled with an array of books in different styles of stacking. There were also two spaces within the bookcase that had room for a wooden monkey and a photo frame of his family, along with a baseball trophy. Certificates hung on the nearest wall to the door, and a wooden coat stand stood to the left of the door, carefully positioned not to get knocked over when the door opened. A deer head on a wooden shield hung on the wall.

Morag and Dougie entered the room, and there was a pause in silence before anything was said. Morag raised her right hand and gave the sheriff a little excited wave. "Hello, Sheriff."

"Hello, Morag."

"Sheriff."

"Yes, Morag."

Another slight pause followed. "This is Detective Dougie Woodbridge."

The Sheriff looks at Dougie and does a casual wave at Dougie. Then looks back at Morag.
"Thank you Morag, Morag."
"Yes, Sheriff?"

Steve points at her hair. "You have a..." Keeps pointing at her hair but he can't get his words out of his mouth.

"Have a what? Sheriff."
"You have a pen?"
"A pen sheriff?"
"Yes it's stuck in your hair, look..."

Morag looks at her hair and then notices it, and she remembers, it's all coming back to her now.

"Oh yes, so I do" Morag moves her hand towards and starts trying to get it out.

Dougie looks and smiles at them both. There's a stone silence as Morag tries to untwine the pen away from her hair, yet can't do it instantly then looks at the Sheriff and lets go of her hair. "Okay Sheriff, well I should get back to my desk."

"Thank you Morag."
Morag looks at Dougie, "Detective Woodbridge."
"Thank you Morag, it's been nice meeting you."

She gives him a little nod and looks at the Sheriff, then turns and awkwardly leaves. The Sheriff looks at Dougie and smiles and then shows his hand to a chair in front of his desk. "Take a seat Dougie."

Dougie walks the remaining distance to the vacant green leather chair (same chair type as Steve's) that's sat on the other side of the

Sheriff's desk. He walks over to it, puts his briefcase down and pulls the chair back slightly so he can comfortably sit down.

When he's sat comfortably the Sheriff takes his hat off and puts it down on the desk. And puts his hands together and rests his arms and elbows on the desk.

Dougie holds his coffee and occasionally sips it. They look at each other and smile with a slight pause in silence before Steve starts the conversation. "Welcome to Emerald Cove, how are you settling in?"

"Very well thank you considering this is my second day here. It's a beautiful town."

Steve smiles, yet that smile quickly turns into a more serious, concerned face.
"Thank you, it is beautiful, yet don't let that deceive you. A lot of strange things happen in this place." The Sheriff gives him a stare as

Dougie smiles back and nods, the Sheriff then takes his focus away and looks to the drawer (on his desk) to the right of him and opens it .
He pulls out a detective badge and gun with a brown holster. And then hands it over to him. "Dougie, do you mind if I ask you a personal question?"

"Of course sir, I'll try my best to answer it."

The sheriff holds that concerned look. "Have you had breakfast yet?"

Dougie looks up and thinks. "Vaguely?"

"You had a vague breakfast?" The Sheriff casually picks up his hat and puts it on his head and then stands up and walks around his desk and past Dougie towards the door and then stops and stares. "Well that's not good for anyone. One thing you need to know about this town is, you can't have a vague breakfast! Right, come with me, I'm going to take you for the best breakfast in town, I'll fill you when we get there."

They both walk out of the room (Dougie puts his mug on the desk and picks up his briefcase) and down the corridor with Steve in front. The walls of the corridor have medium dark wood. With various posters and pictures on them that you associate a police station with. They both go back towards the reception area where the receptionist looks like she's in heaps of bother and frustration. Steve looks back at Dougie, "How's the unpacking going?"

"So, so."

Sheriff Steve Hughes looks back and stops as he can't quite get around what he's seeing by Morag. "What the hell?"

In front of Morag are two men wearing overalls, standing by them is a massive dark brown oak dining table. One man is holding a clipboard signing sheet.

Morag can't hold her frustration, "I will repeat this again. Why would I want you to bring the table into my workplace when I want it at my house? I said I would sign for it here, but I didn't say to bring it here!"

Harry the workman is confused, "So you don't want us to bring in the chairs?"

Morag stamps her foot on the floor in frustration. "No! I don't want you to bring in the chairs!"

Tina's Diner.

Tina's Diner is a typical "American Diner" split into three main parts. The left side of the room has wooden tables with a white finish and seats all around them, full of customers.

The middle is a long rectangular area that sits in the middle of the room, this is where the two waitresses are, and they prepare the food, there's coffee machines and fizzy drinks machines.

It's a mini open kitchen area, this area is separated by a food top counter area that goes all the way around so the customers can sit on the stools by it. On the counters sits some raised cake stands with freshly prepared cakes wrapped in cling film. There's also a shelved hot plate stand in a glass style cabinet for warm foods. This has pies and other various warm baked goods inside. On the counter there's also yellow and red plastic sauce pots that you get typically for ketchup and mustard. As well as salt, pepper, and two types of sugar pots . A fake plant is also on there, newspapers in random places for customers to read.

There's four customers sitting on stools around this area either side eating pies and breakfast. All the customers and staff in the room look over the age of thirty. The waitresses can get in and out from the counter area at either end, by a hip height moving flap door, so they can carry food and drinks. The right side of the room has wooden tables with a white finish and seats all around them full of customers. Apart from a couple of tables.

The front door (that the customers get in and out), is by a cigarette machine. And there's big glass panel windows either side of the door with long red hanging curtains in front of them.

Dougie and Sheriff Steve Hughes walked into the diner. Above the door, there was a large green-lit "EXIT" sign in capital letters, serving as an emergency exit indicator.

The walls inside the diner were adorned with beige wooden panels running from top to bottom, neatly fixed side by side. White and red posters displaying various food and drink deals adorned the walls. The floor featured a checkered pattern of black and red tiles.

One of the two waitresses, Camile, was engaged in a conversation with a customer at the counter. The man wore a red and black checked lumberjack jumper, blue denim jeans, and black boots. His short hair was black, and he sported black stubble.

Camile handed over the bill to the man, which amounted to $8.24. On the table in front of him, there was an empty white plate with a patterned blue trim. The plate bore traces of purple, blue, and red fruit stains, evidence of a pie that had been enjoyed. Next to the plate, a mug contained a few drops of black coffee.

"Here's your bill, Stan," Camile said as she handed over a white piece of paper displaying the total.

Stan examined the bill, smiled, and nodded. He then raised his index finger, signalling Camile to wait for a moment while he fumbled to retrieve his wallet. Stan shifted on his stool, first reaching into his left pocket, only to realise his wallet wasn't there. He then checked his right pocket and pulled out a bulky brown leather wallet, filled more with receipts than money. From it, he took out a ten-dollar bill, returning the wallet to his right pocket. He handed the ten-dollar bill to Camile, who smiled back with patience and affection.

The whole transaction took longer than necessary. Sheriff Steve Hughes walked through the front door of Tina's Diner, followed by Dougie. They made their way to the left of Stan and waited to place their orders.

"Keep the change, Camile. Again, that's the best Huckleberry pie in the whole of America," Stan said as he prepared to leave.

"Thank you, Stan. I'm glad you think so," Camile replied.

Stan stood up, wiped his mouth, and turned his attention to Steve and Dougie. He smiled at Dougie and greeted Steve with enthusiasm.

"Hiya Steve, see ya later, Camile."

"Bye Stan," Camile replied.

Steve then looked at Camile, and Camile smiled back, wondering what Steve would like to order. Stan exited through the front door.

"Hiya, Camile. Can I have some of that famous Huckleberry Pie?" Steve inquired.

Camile nodded as she noted down the order on her notepad.

"With a waffle and some whipped cream. And a black coffee," Steve added.

Camile continued jotting down the order and turned her attention to Dougie.

"Of course," she said, briefly looking at Dougie while writing the order. "And what can I get for your friend?"

"I'll have the same, please," Dougie replied.

Camile smiled affectionately, pointing to a free
set of tables and red chairs.

"If you want to take a seat, I'll bring your order
over shortly," she suggested.

Steve tapped his hand on the counter in
satisfaction and began walking away.

"Thanks, Camile," he said.

Steve and Dougie found their way to a table
indicated by Camile, taking seats across from
each other. Steve removed his Sheriff hat and
unclipped his police radio from the chest pocket
of his jacket, placing it on the table. They
exchanged a brief glance before Dougie took a
moment to observe the diner's decor.

"Nice place," Dougie remarked.

Sheriff Steve nodded and briefly scanned the
room with his eyes.

"I've been coming here forever, it seems. The woman who owns this place certainly knows how to make a recipe for pie," he commented. He paused to look around. "It doesn't look like she's here this morning, otherwise I would have introduced you."

Camile emerged from the kitchen/till area, carrying a tray with two red mugs turned upside down on white saucers, each with a spoon beside it. A pot of coffee was also on the tray. She approached their table with a professional demeanour, setting the mugs down one by one and turning them over. Camile then poured coffee into Dougie's mug and then into Steve's.

"Here's your coffee, boys," she said with a warm smile.

After Camile had placed the mugs and poured the coffee, both Steve and Dougie thanked her. Camile left the coffee pot on the table, near the ketchup, mustard, sugar, and salt containers, and smiled at them before Steve introduced her to Dougie. "Thank you, Camile. Camile, I would like you to meet our new Detective, Dougie Woodbridge," Steve said.

"Nice to meet you, Dougie," Camile replied, extending her hand for a handshake, which Dougie accepted. They exchanged smiles, and Camile briefly rested her hand on Dougie's shoulder before walking away, promising a bigger slice of pie for the compliment.

Dougie looked at Steve and remarked, "I could get used to a place like this if all you have to do is say nice things to get a bigger piece of pie."

Steve chuckled and asked, "If only the rest of the world was that easy, hey?"

"Absolutely. I think for now, I'll just quit while I'm ahead and stick with buttering up waitresses for a bigger slice of pie."

Steve changed the topic, asking about Dougie's adjustment to the slower pace of life compared to New York.

"How are you finding the slower life here compared to New York?"

"I'm looking forward to getting used to it. I was never one for the city. I would much prefer to bring up my daughter here than in a place where you get the option to make so many bad choices in one day. It's like a risk assessor's worst nightmare. And if you're a father, that's what you end up becoming."

The Sheriff nodded in agreement, picked up his coffee, and took a sip. "I hear that. Bringing up kids anywhere isn't a walk in the park."

Dougie also nodded in agreement, and Steve took another sip of his coffee. Dougie stirred his coffee with a spoon a few times, tapped the spoon on the edge of the cup, and then took a sip, visibly pleased with the taste.

"Oh my, that's incredible coffee! Ask me again how I'm settling into the place," Dougie said, keeping the coffee mug in his hand.

Steve chuckled and asked, "How are you settling in?"

As they enjoyed their coffee, another waitress passed by with two plates of food. One of them commented, "I can't wait to taste the pie!"

"I reckon you'll do okay around here, Dougie," Steve remarked, taking a sip of his coffee.

Dougie took a big sip and held the cup to his mouth for a while. Steve watched him, and then they both heard a voice on the police radio. It was Morag calling in.

"Sir, sir, Sheriff Steve Hughes, are you there? Sir, are you there, over? It's Morag over."

Steve and Dougie kept their coffee mugs at their mouths, listening. Steve eventually put down his mug and picked up the radio, clicking the button to acknowledge Morag's call.

"Receiving, over. How may I help, Morag?"

"Sheriff Steve Hughes, we need you at Emerald Cove Beach by the car park. A body has been found."

Steve's eyes widened in response to the urgent message. Dougie, using both hands, quickly finished his coffee. Camile arrived with their food, and Steve got up from his seat, attaching the radio to his jacket pocket. He left money on the table and even had a bite of his waffle before leaving.

Dougie, on the other hand, offered a polite thank you and goodbye gesture before exiting with Steve.

Chapter Three: Spew.

At Emerald Cove Beach, they arrived to find a
grim scene. A police officer named Chet Ramis
had cordoned off an area around a body that had
been wrapped in thick plastic sheeting. The body
was positioned between the shoreline and the
car park, secured with black grip ties and clear
wire. Chet appeared visibly disturbed, trying to
avoid looking at the body.

Two onlookers, a husband and wife in their
sixties, stood nearby, the woman in tears while
the man consoled her. Officer Jonathan Davies,
a man in his late fifties, approached Steve and
Dougie, gesturing for them to come over. They
exchanged introductions.

"Nice to meet you, Dougie," Jonathan said, shaking Dougie's hand.

"And nice to meet you too," Dougie replied.

Jonathan then returned to reviewing his notes, occasionally flipping through his notepad while maintaining a professional demeanour. Steve inquired about Chet's reaction.

"Could you enlighten me as to what's causing Chet to feel ill? That man has seen his share of dead bodies, and I've never seen him react like this."

Jonathan briefly glanced at Chet, then back at Steve and Dougie before refocusing on his notes.

"The first thing I can tell you is that forensics has been called in by Morag to come down here."

Steve nodded as he absorbed the information.

"And what I'm about to tell you next is rather disturbing," Jonathan continued, gesturing toward Chet with his pen and notepad. "Hence why Chet looks the way he does. Not long ago, I was in the same state. And if I were you guys, I wouldn't want to go anywhere near that body until the lab has finished processing it."

Both Dougie and Steve were left speechless, their expressions growing increasingly mystified and disturbed by what they were hearing. Steve finally asked, "So, what kind of case are we dealing with here, Jonathan?"

Jonathan locked eyes with them and took his time with his response. "It's the case where your arms and legs have been severed, swapped, and sewn back on. After that, the person was wrapped in plastic with zip ties and left on a beach."

The shocking revelation left both officers stunned. They covered their mouths and foreheads, grappling with disbelief and a deep sense of disturbance. Jonathan suggested, "I'll give you guys some time to process this."

Steve stepped away briefly, needing a moment to collect his thoughts, while the other two officers were left in a state of shock and introspection.

Dougie's Driveway.

Dougie turned the key in his car's ignition, shutting off the engine. He took a deep breath and rested his head on the steering wheel. In the background, a door slammed shut, followed by a knock on his car window. Dougie looked up to see his daughter standing there. He gestured with his index finger, indicating for her to wait a moment. Undoing his seatbelt, he opened the driver's door but remained seated.

His daughter appeared concerned, and the family dog, Bear, was on a leash beside her. Ariel could see that her dad was clearly exhausted. "Are you okay, Dad? I heard you come into the driveway. You've been sitting there a long time."

Dougie confirmed, "It's not been a good first day."

Ariel showed a semi-concerned expression. "What happened? Did you have a hard time for being late?"

Dougie managed a slight grin and began moving to exit his car. He quickly looked away, grabbed his suitcase, and stepped out of the car as his daughter made way for him. Once fully out of the car, he shut the door. "We'll save it for another time. Are you taking Bear for a walk?"

"Yeah, we're going to go in the fields behind our house, probably up near the woods and walk back. We haven't tried it yet. I just thought I'd check if you're okay first."

Dougie leaned in and gave his daughter a kiss on the cheek. "Sounds good. I'll meet you up there, and you can tell me about your first day at school. I'll just pop my briefcase in, put on some trainers, and get a glass of water."

"Okay, catch you in a bit," Ariel said. She looked at Bear, patted the side of her hip, and said, "Come on, Bear." Bear looked up at Ariel and then started walking alongside her.

Shepperton Field.

Dougie walked in his trainers and red coat along a path by the edge of the ploughed field. Numerous bird species were scattered around the area. As Dougie approached nearly halfway up the field, he could see the opening of the woods. He continued walking but couldn't spot anyone. His gaze swept across the field and then back to the woods, where he suddenly saw a dog that looked like Bear emerging from the edge of the woods.

As the dog stepped onto the field, it collapsed in a heap. Panic washed over Dougie's face, and he began sprinting. A naked woman followed, running out of the same opening as the dog. She appeared to be chasing the dog, her head moving rapidly as she scanned for the dog. Upon seeing the dog on the ground, she fell to her knees, emitting piercing, disturbing screams. It was as if she were seeing her own hands and body for the first time.

Dougie sprinted as fast as he could. The woman's piercing screams seemed never-ending, interrupted only by brief breaths. Ariel looked up and saw Dougie running towards her. Her initial relief was short-lived amid the shock. She stopped screaming and said, "Dad? Dad! Bear's dead!"

Dougie looked at her, completely bewildered and scared. "Ariel?"

His daughter now appeared as a middle-aged woman in her forties, resembling Ariel but crying beside her dead dog Bear. The dog looked like a withered corpse on the ground, identifiable only by the red collar. Dougie struggled to recognize either of them.

Ariel appeared distraught and disoriented, overwhelmed by a mix of emotions. Dougie looked at the dog on the floor as he fell to his knees to console his daughter. She held him tightly, her tears and snot staining her father's clothing.

Dougie removed his coat and draped it over Ariel's shoulders. "Thank you," she said as she continued to shake from adrenaline. Ariel put on the jacket and struggled to speak. "What's happened to us, Dad? Why is Bear dead? What's happened to me?"

Dougie was puzzled. "I honestly don't know." He placed his hands on either side of her face and locked eyes with her. They shared a moment of silence as he studied her. "I promise you, I will find out what happened to you. Can you tell me anything about what happened there?"

Dougie withdrew his hands from her face, and Ariel, looking bewildered and scared, attempted to recall the events, her body still shaking from shock. "I remember Bear spotted a rabbit and chased it into the woods," she began, her voice shaky. "I started to go into the woods to find Bear, but I can't remember being in there. I just came out this way, and Bear was dead on the ground, and I wasn't wearing any clothes."

She paused, trying to remember more, but her expression turned blank and filled with fear. She wiped snot onto her hand and then onto her thigh, resting her hand on the ground. "Dad, why can't I remember being in there? What's happening to me?" Ariel started sobbing and breathing erratically. "Why the heck is Bear like that?"

Dougie embraced her, hugging her close. He rested his chin on her head as they held each other, and he occasionally kissed her head. "Just breathe, Ariel, concentrate on your breathing," he urged. "Deep breath."

Ariel attempted to focus on her breathing, taking deep breaths. "And breathe out..." Dougie instructed, and Ariel complied. "Well done."

Dougie looked into Ariel's eyes as they broke the hug. "I've got a plan, and the first step is to get you home." He began removing his shoes and socks.

"What are you doing, Dad?"

"Here, put on these socks. You can't walk home like that." Dougie handed his socks to her, and Ariel began to put them on. Dougie then unbuckled his belt and removed his trousers, passing them to Ariel. "And these, put them on."

"If anyone asks why I'm in boxers, just say I've had a bit too much to drink again. It's been a long day at work. We'll keep walking. You won't need to say anything else or do anything else." Dougie handed his trainers to Ariel.

Once Ariel had changed, which took longer than usual due to her continued adrenaline-induced shaking, they stood up. Dougie looked at the remains of Bear, tears streaming down Ariel's face. "I can't wrap my head around it."

Dougie took a deep breath and silently observed the remains for a moment before speaking. "You don't need to wrap your head around anything right now, except getting your slightly inebriated father home." He put his arm around Ariel. "Come on, let's get you back."

Chapter Four: Shitshow Cocktail.

On the front doorstep of Dougie and Ariel's house, Dougie needed Ariel's help. "Inside my jacket, Ariel, are the front door keys. Can you pass them to me?" Ariel nodded and searched his pockets for the keys. Meanwhile, over Ariel's shoulder, Dougie noticed his neighbour on the other side of the street, standing in his front garden, saluting next to the American flag. He was wearing a bingo hat, a white vest, house slippers, and shorts held up with braces. He had a pipe in his mouth, a newspaper in one hand, and was staring into space with a bit of drool coming down his corner lip.

"Here you go, Dad," Ariel passed him the keys, still looking distraught and in shock.

"Thanks, hon." Dougie took the keys and moved toward the front door, unlocking it. He let his daughter go inside first, then followed her and closed the door behind them.

Ten minutes later, there was a knock on the front door. Sheriff Steve Hughes stood there. Dougie arrived at the door to let him in. They didn't say anything to each other at the doorway; Dougie just gestured for him to come in. They both walked into the kitchen. Not long after, Steve's wife entered the front door and joined them in the kitchen, where Ariel was sitting in a dressing gown, sipping a hot drink at the table.

"I thought it would be best if Sandy came over. I thought Ariel could use having a woman around in these circumstances," Steve explained.

"I hope you don't mind. I can leave in an instant if you feel it's inappropriate," Sandy added.

Dougie insisted, "It's a good idea. Please stay. Take a seat." Dougie directed Sandy to a chair next to Ariel. They all sat down except for Dougie, who remained standing. They sat in silence for a while. "Would you like a coffee?" Dougie asked.

"If you have a pot going, I'll take a cup. You know those days when you don't get around to finishing a cup of coffee? Today, so far, has been one of those," Steve replied.

"Sandy?"

"I'm okay. If I have another, I won't stop peeing!"

Dougie retrieved a red mug from the cupboard and poured Steve a coffee, then placed it on a coaster in front of him on the table. "Here you go. If you need anything to go with it, you should find it on the table."

"Thanks, Dougie," Steve said as he added sugar to his coffee. Dougie didn't take a seat but moved back to where the kitchen counter was and leaned against it. The group remained in the same room but didn't speak for about a minute. During that time, each of them took individual moments to glance at Ariel, who continued to stare into space in shock, occasionally shaking from adrenaline.

"I've sent a team up to the area you suggested. Morag will keep me updated when they're done. It's up to you both if you want to get Ariel checked over before she has a wash. I'll leave you both to discuss this," Steve finally said.

Dougie looked at Steve, and Ariel continued to gaze into space. "I just don't know how much more I can put her through right now," Dougie said, his concern evident as he looked at Ariel.

"There's no immediate hurry. She's back safe
now, and that's all that matters."

Emerald Cove Doctors Surgery.

The next day, Dougie sat in the waiting room at Emerald Cove Doctors Surgery, waiting for Ariel as she underwent a check-up with Doctor Ralph Essien. His attention was caught by a patient in the waiting room with an eye patch covering her left eye and a broken right arm. She sniffled into a polka dot handkerchief with her good hand and then glanced at Dougie.

To her left was another woman, approximately forty years old, with a noticeable hunch in her back. She wore glasses and sat uncomfortably in her chair, occasionally making grunting noises and shifting from one butt cheek to the other to ease the discomfort.

Dougie's gaze shifted to the corner of the waiting room, where a small collection of toys lay, organised for children. However, they seemed untouched and unused for quite some time. After a while, he heard a door open and watched as two people walked out.

Fifteen minutes later, Dougie was in the car, with Ariel in the passenger seat, driving through an estate in Emerald Cove. It appeared to be very quiet, with only a few people walking their dogs on the sidewalks or tending to their gardens. After a minute, Dougie turned into Durnball Street and parked outside number seventeen.

As soon as he parked, the front door of Sandy and Steve's house opened, and Sandy stood in the doorway, waving toward the car. Dougie looked at Sandy, then at Ariel, who was looking at Sandy. "Are you sure you're going to be okay spending a few hours with Sandy while I go to work?" Ariel nodded but didn't look at Dougie.

He wanted to reassure her that she didn't have to do this. "If you feel uncomfortable with this, you don't have to. We can go home; I won't go to work."

"Honestly, Dad, it's okay," Ariel replied, opening the car door. "Just go and get some answers." She looked at her father and held his hand.

"I love you, Ariel."

"I love you too, Dad." Ariel got out of the car, closed the door behind her, and started walking down the path toward the front door of Sandy and Steve's house. As she did, she looked back for another glimpse, and Sandy greeted her with a hug.

They both waved to Dougie, and then they entered the house. Once they were inside, Dougie rested his head on the steering wheel, taking a moment to gather himself mentally.

Emerald Cove Police Station.

Dougie knocked on the door of Sheriff Steve Hughes' office and waited for a response. Shortly after, Steve came to the door, holding a cordless telephone. Steve didn't say anything but gestured for Dougie to come in and take a seat while he continued his phone call.

"Okay, leave that information with me to soak in for a moment, and I'll either be there or someone else will at some point today," Steve said into the phone. "Okay, thanks, Irene. Anything else pops up, let me know, yeah?" Dougie could hear Irene's voice on the other end. "Thank you, speak soon, Irene."

Steve hung up the phone and placed it on his desk. He removed his hat and placed it on the desk, then ran his hand through his hair. "How is Ariel?"

"She's still older."

"Yesterday was a pretty messed up day, wasn't it?"

"It was a complete disaster," Dougie replied.

"Irene is one of the people dealing with the body that was found yesterday," Steve continued. "According to them, inside some of the parts of the arms and legs, some tissue and bones have been removed and filled with foreign objects as replacements."

"You mean?" Dougie began, his voice filled with shock.

"She didn't say what those objects are yet."

"Permission to talk out of turn, Sheriff."

"Granted."

"What kind of town have you brought me into here, Sheriff? My daughter is never going to be the same again, and you've got people swapping body parts and filling them up with jelly beans. If you don't start giving me some straight answers right now, I'm going to throw you into those woods as my own personal guinea pig just to see what happens." Dougie's frustration and anger were evident as he looked at Steve.

Steve wasn't angry with Dougie. In fact, he wanted to be straightforward and provide as much information as he could. However, at this moment, he could only divulge so much. "The woods make people age, most of the time people come back around thirty years older. We don't know why, as people can't remember."

"You mean there have been more like Ariel?"

"That's correct."

"How many more?"

"Does it matter?" Steve inquired.

"A little, yeah! What the heck do you mean? Of course, it matters!"

"We've had the brightest minds venture in there to try to find out what's happening. They never remember what they find inside. They remember nothing. Black-suited companies have given up trying to figure out what it is. They've thrown electronics in there to investigate, but it doesn't work, or it doesn't return. They've sent personnel in there, and they come back older and forgetful, or too old to cross the line and live."

"So why isn't it fenced off?"

"Do you know how many kids will jump a fence to be a grown-up?"

"Do you know how many kids will jump a fence to be a grown-up?"

"You're kidding?"

"More than without a fence, we did the data."

"In the end, it was taken down and replaced with signs for private land, but no one owns it. It seems to deter more people that way. We've basically been left to it now. Occasionally, we get a suit up here from time to time, believing they've got a new way to solve it. Most of the time, it seems like they've been putting their manpower into somewhere or someone else."

"Or maybe they've found out what it is and just aren't letting you know. Have you thought of that?"

"I'll add it to the theory pile."

"So what the heck am I going to do about my daughter?"

"Tell her you love her and be a father."

"And if this were your daughter, would you go to any length you could to find out what did this to her? And then find a way to fix it if you found there was a way to fix it? Or to stop this from happening to anyone else again?"

Steve looks at Dougie and takes a deep breath. "Dougie, we've had every type come here saying they're going to work out what those woods are. Every type, the road you're considering right now, and I understand why, and I understand that I'm probably not the man who's going to talk you out of what you're thinking of doing. But all roads lead to you remembering nothing, and you'll probably have no hair left on your head when you come back, if you come back. And your daughter needs you here, to comfort her in what are the scariest moments of her life. Not there, in those woods! Because if you're gone, who has she got then?"

"So what, I'm just supposed to tell her you walked into the wrong woods, now you're old enough to get married?! Screw you, Steve, screw you! I'm supposed to protect her, I'm supposed to understand what she is going through and make it go away."

The phone rings, and Steve looks at Dougie. He doesn't want the conversation to end but still needs to answer the phone and see what is happening. "You stay there and hold that thought." Steve looks at the machine, and he can see that it's Morag waiting to get through; the red light is flashing. Steve pushes the button, and Morag is on the loudspeaker. "Yes, Morag."

"Sheriff."

"Yes, Morag."

"Sheriff, I was wondering if you could help me? I'm having furniture problems."

"Furniture problems?"

Dougie gets up and starts to leave the room, but Steve tries to stop him. "Dougie, stay." Dougie looks at him and then leaves the room.

Morag continues, "I need you to ban them."

"Dougie, stay." Steve looks at Dougie, but he doesn't want to leave the conversation. "Ban the furniture?"

"No, the people who deliver it, they're here again."

"Why are they here?"

As Dougie walks through the police station, he notices several delivery men holding items ten feet long.

Morag can be heard shouting, "BUT WE DIDN'T ORDER FISH TANKS!"

Chapter Five: Prolonged Coffee.

Steve drives through Stainpoe Avenue, passing a couple of cars before parking outside Emerald Junior School. He turns off the ignition, grabs what he needs, takes the keys out of the car, and opens the door.

Moments later, the door is held open for him in the principal's office. Principal Marge Ragnick has grey hair, blue-square glasses, colourful earrings, a mauve turtleneck jumper, black trousers, and flat shoes. Marge sits behind her desk and welcomes Dougie to sit down on one of the chairs on the other side of the desk.

The room is filled with various accolades, paperwork, stationery, and potted plants. Dougie scans the room.

"Please take a seat, Detective," Marge smiles.

Dougie raises his eyebrows, "Thank you," and takes a seat, slightly adjusting the chair to the left before doing so.

"I'm just following up on a few things related to a case. I was wondering if you could help with a few questions, as you know the students at this school, their parents, and possibly some playground talk," Dougie says.

"I'll do my best to answer your questions."

"Are you local to this area?"

"That's correct."

"Have you been living here for long?"

"About eight years."

"And how old are you?"

"Fourteen."

Dougie looks up from his notepad, straight at
Marge, just to make sure he heard that right.
He also wants to see Marge's reaction if she has
realised what she said. He notices her attempt
to correct her answer. "Kidding, have you seen
these greys? That's what kids will do to you! I'm
forty-four."

Dougie smiles and jots down her corrected age
on his notepad. "And how long have you been a
teacher here?"

"Sixteen months."

"And within that time, how many children have left this school and moved to another before the end of their school year?"

"What do you mean?"

"How many children have not completed their education here by the time they're supposed to? Either by moving to another school, passing away, or due to other unusual events, such as not receiving an explanation as to why they've left."

"I think it's twenty-seven."

"Twenty-seven?"

"Does that number seem strange to you?"

"In what sense?" Marge isn't entirely sure how the question is directed.

"Is it usual for a school to lose that many children within that time frame?"

"It's a big school, and five to six years of their life here is not always a guarantee."

"In what sense?"

"In the early part of the kids' lives, parents, especially first-time parents, tend to move around a bit to find a more permanent home for the next stage of their lives, rather than this stage. But to answer your previous question, I would say the numbers are a little high."

Dougie doesn't ask any further questions about that. Instead, he jots down her answer. "Do you have a list of their names? The students who left and their previous contact information?"

"Sure, I can get that for you." Marge calls reception via the telephone. She waits for the receptionist to pick up. "Hello, Mrs. Ragnick."

"Hi, Renee. Could you get a list of names of the students who have left before completing their school year and their previous contact information? Going back eighteen months. This information is for Detective Woodbridge, so I need this fast-tracked as quickly as possible."

"I'll be as quick as possible."

"Thanks, Renee." Marge hangs up the call and looks at Dougie, ready for a follow-up question. "Could you tell me if the children here ever mention the woods up by Shepperton field?"

Marge's facial expression changes slightly. "A few times."

"And what type of things do they say?"

"You know, not to go in there because of the monsters. And then they talk about what monsters they think are in there."

"And do these kids ever say that they're considering going inside there?"

"Sometimes."

"Are you aware of anyone from this school who has been there?"

"I couldn't say for certain."

"Do you have any suspicions?"

"Sorry, is there something I should know about these woods? Has something happened?"

"Do you have any suspicions?"

"Nothing that I could say with any certainty. However, if I get you those names, and if any, in particular, stand out, I will highlight them for you."

Dougie looks into Marge's eyes. "That'll do just fine."

Two hours later, Dougie is sitting in Tina's Diner, looking over at Camile as she brings an extra-large piece of pie and a mug of coffee. "Thanks, Camile," Dougie smiles as she places it on the table.

"You're welcome. So, I see you're not with Steve today. We must have done something right for you to come back on your own?"

"I guess you could say maybe I didn't give it a fair shot after leaving early last time. In that sense, it would be unfair for me not to come back."

"Still the gentleman, I see." Camile has finished setting the items on Dougie's table, so now she's off to serve the next customer. Camile smiles and starts to walk away.

Dougie smiles back and then picks up a tablespoon, cutting into his blueberry pie. He scoops it onto the spoon and brings it to his mouth, taking a bite. With his other hand, he opens a small folder containing the list of students who left before completing their school year, with dates spanning back eighteen months. Straight away, Dougie notices that a large number of these names are highlighted.

Dougie puts his spoon onto his plate and begins to look further. He soon realises that only five are not highlighted. Once he reaches the end of that information, he notices that he's been given some separate sheets with information. The list includes all the children who have left early, going back five years. These are not highlighted, but the information is there.

Twenty minutes pass, and Dougie is yet to have another piece of pie. He's engrossed in reviewing all the names. Using a pen, he circles anything and everything that seems odd to him, occasionally writing a side note. Camile walks by and notices that Dougie hasn't taken another bite of his pie, but she doesn't comment, as Dougie seems busy with work.

A minute later, however, Dougie looks up and puts his pen down. He takes a big gulp of coffee and looks around the room. He then looks over to Camile and observes other people in the room. Inside the room, there are a few tables filled with three or four people sitting at them, and a couple of people, including Stan, sitting on stools. Dougie puts his coffee down and begins to eat the rest of his pie.

Five minutes later, Dougie has finished his pie and his coffee. Camile comes over and asks, "Can I get you a refill, Detective?"

Dougie looks up, "Just a couple of pieces of pie to go, a big slice of chocolate cake, and the bill."

"Do you want them wrapped individually?"

"Yes, please."

"I'll get on that now."

"Camile."

"Yes?"

"Before you do, can I ask you something pretty random?"

"It wouldn't be the first time I've been asked that, so fire away."

"Why is it that the last couple of times I've been here, I haven't seen any families with young children? The place always seems to have older folks."

"Probably just because it's been school days the days you've been here."

"Possibly."

"Why do you ask?"

"Just an observation. With the cakes and pies you have here, I thought kids would be screaming to get their parents to bring them here."

"You'd think, right?"

"Also, you're pretty local, right?"

"Sure am."

Dougie looks at some quick notes he has. "Have you ever heard of these people or the family names: Kiera Martial, Tricia Kane, Frenkie Vaughn, and Santi Casemiro?"

Camile looks at Dougie, unsure how to respond. She would like to help, but she can't. "Sorry, Dougie, I hope it's not important."

Dougie shrugs his shoulders. "Nothing important.
I just thought those are quite memorable
names." Dougie tries not to give too much away.

"I'll get you those items." Camile smiles and
walks away to the open kitchen to slice up and
box some cake and pie. Camile picks out a box
and looks over to Dougie to see if he's still
looking at her. Then she looks away and goes to
the cake stand to get the cake. Dougie continues
to look at his notes and then puts them in his
pocket.

Chapter Six: Bag of Cake.

Dougie leaves Tina's Diner with a bag of cake and pie and walks to his car. He pushes the button on his key, which automatically unlocks the car doors before he reaches the car. He opens the door, sits in his seat, and places his bag of food and information file on the passenger seat next to him. Dougie puts his key into the ignition of the car but doesn't turn it on just yet. Instead, he takes out the file of information again. As he gets the file, he notices a post-it note on top of the chocolate cake box, which is now open.

Dougie looks down at the bright orange post-it note. The note has writing on it, "The Martials are at table 11." Dougie continues to stare at the note for a moment. After about ten seconds, Dougie reaches down, pulls the note away from the cake box, and brings it closer to him. Dougie continues to look at the writing and then looks back at Tina's Diner.

Dougie tries to remember what table number he was sitting at and the layout of the table settings, as well as what the people sitting at that table looked like. For now, Dougie stays in his car and waits for them to come out of the building.

Fifteen minutes later, Dougie notices a family he believes was sitting at table eleven. The family has three members: an elderly man and woman who appear to be in their seventies, and another woman who looks to be in her late thirties or early forties. Dougie doesn't approach the family; instead, he watches them return to their vehicle. It's not long before they're all in the car and heading away from Tina's Diner.

After about fifteen minutes of driving, the vehicle Dougie has been following heads up a farm track. Dougie decides to follow them, and the track is long with various potholes along the way. Some of the potholes have been recently filled, but many remain.

Dougie starts to lose sight of the vehicle but figures they can't be too far ahead. He follows the track to the end and takes a right turn, even though a left turn is available. The right turn leads to another track lined with tall fir trees. This track continues for about a minute, ending at a secluded bungalow with the vehicle Dougie has been following parked outside, which he believes belongs to the Martials.

The lights are on inside the building, so Dougie parks outside the bungalow and gets out of his car. He walks up to the blue door and knocks on the brass knocker. Dougie notices a twitch at the curtain, and shortly after, an elderly man opens the door and looks at Dougie.

"Mr. Martial, I presume?"

The elderly man looks at Dougie, his expression resigned.

Ten minutes later, Dougie is sitting in the lounge of the Martials' home, drinking a cup of mint leaf tea. "Very refreshing, thank you."

"It's always nicer straight from the garden," comments Mrs. Martial. "It's like the bush that keeps giving."

Dougie smiles and looks at a painting above the sofa where Mr. and Mrs. Martial are sitting. Above the sofa is a picture of a white chair in front of a grandfather clock. Dougie becomes transfixed by the painting. As he looks closer, it appears that something is trying to emerge from the door of the clock.

He tries to continue the conversation, but in the next moment, he's sitting on the chair in the painting. Then, within the same moment, he's back in the room with the Martials in their bungalow. Dougie doesn't try to overthink what just happened; instead, he asks a question.

"The reason I'm here is about your daughter, Kiera."

Mr. and Mrs. Martial look at Dougie, trying to act surprised, especially Mrs. Martial. "Oh, really?"

"What has she done?" said Mrs. Martial.

Dougie seemed unable to answer the question. Instead, he continued to look around the room. On the floor, an apple appeared that wasn't there before.

Dougie stared at the apple on the floor for an extended period. The apple began to spin, clockwise and then anticlockwise after a few turns, repeating this motion until it stopped.

When a pencil-sized hole appeared in the apple, Dougie focused on this hole.

Dougie remained fixated on the hole in the apple, ignoring everything else in the room for several minutes. After some time had passed, the apple lifted by itself and came closer to Dougie's eyeline. He continued to focus solely on the hole in the apple. Inside the hole, he began to see an image of a clock in his living room, though he wasn't sure why this image was appearing.

Dougie concentrated on the clock in his lounge and then felt himself wake up in his lounge chair. He glanced at the clock, which read 03:35 AM, and felt a breeze brush past his right ear. Dougie stood up and looked around his lounge, wondering what had just happened. As he walked out of the lounge, he noticed that his front door was open.

Puzzled, Dougie walked to the front door and looked outside. He saw his neighbour across the street, standing in his front garden, saluting next to the American flag. The neighbour was wearing a bingo hat, a white vest, house slippers, a dressing gown, and shorts held up with braces. He had a pipe in his mouth and held a newspaper in the other hand, staring into space.

Dougie walked over to the man and stood in front of him, observing him for an extended period. The neighbour didn't seem to fully acknowledge him; instead, he made random noises as he sucked air and shifted his spit to the back of his mouth. Dougie looked down at the newspaper, which was on page eleven. On that page, there was a partially completed crossword puzzle, with only one answer filled in.

Dougie stared at the newspaper page from where he stood. He continued to look at the newspaper until he glanced back at his own house and wondered why his front door was open. Dougie returned to his house, leaving the door open behind him, and walked through the hallway, hearing the ticking of a clock throughout the house. He made his way to his daughter's room.

Upon reaching her door, he noticed that it was open. He fully opened it and looked toward her bed. Ariel wasn't there!

Dougie proceeded to the bathroom and knocked on the door, but there was no response. He opened the door and found that Ariel wasn't there either.

Panicking, Dougie ran toward the front door as fast as his legs could carry him. He headed to his neighbour's house across the street and grabbed the newspaper out of his hand.

Suddenly, Dougie found himself back in a shack, staring at the hole in an apple. As he looked back into the apple, he could see himself running through Shepperton Field, chasing a silhouette near the edge of the woods. Internally, Dougie screamed for his daughter not to enter the woods. As he attempted to scream loudly, the earth beneath his feet crumbled, and his legs buckled due to the unexpected movement of the ground, causing him to fall.

However, the silhouette continued moving closer to the woods. Dougie struggled to crawl against the shifting ground, dragging himself while still holding the newspaper.

"What did she do?" echoed a voice that sounded like Mrs. Martial.

Dougie managed to get up and ran toward the woods, but it was too late; the silhouette had entered the woods before he could reach it. Dougie continued running toward the woods, only metres away.

As Dougie entered the woods, he suddenly found himself back in the shack, looking at the hole in an apple.

Ariel woke up with her headphones in her ears, connected to her phone. She had been listening to music to help her fall asleep. Now that she was awake, she felt quite thirsty, so she decided to go to the kitchen to get a drink.

Before heading to the kitchen, she grabbed her dressing gown hanging on the hook of her bedroom door. She put it on and tied the cord around her waist. Ariel walked out of the room and into the kitchen, still listening to music.

She reached the fridge and opened it, grabbing the blue-top milk by the handle and pulling it out. Ariel placed the milk on the table and then went to the cookie jar in the cupboard, opening it. She brought the cookie jar to the table and sat down on a chair that was already pulled out.

There was a clean glass on the table from breakfast earlier. Ariel picked up the glass and moved it closer. She unscrewed the milk's lid and poured it into the glass, filling it nearly to the top. Ariel leaned down to take a sip of milk without holding the glass, then lifted the lid off the cookie jar.

Ariel peered into the jar before selecting a couple of cookies and placing one double-chocolate chip cookie onto the table. She dunked a quarter of the other cookie into the glass of milk, watching it soften. Ariel took a bite of the softened part before it could fall apart.

She then dipped half of the remaining cookie into the milk and repeated the process. Once there was no more cookie left to dip, she ate the remaining crumbs. Ariel stared into space for a moment as she listened to music before eating the next cookie. She dipped the next one into the milk but this time sucked the milk-soaked biscuit before it crumbled in her mouth.

After finishing her drink, Ariel got up, fetched a couple of slices of bread from the bread bin, and found a plate to put them on. She opened a top kitchen cupboard and retrieved a half-empty jar of peanut butter. Ariel unscrewed the lid and picked up a clean bread knife from the washboard by the kitchen sink.

She spread the peanut butter over both pieces of bread and, once done, returned the lid to the jar, screwing it tightly. Ariel placed the jar back into the cupboard and then licked the remaining peanut butter off the knife before putting it in the sink.

Carrying the plate with her to the kitchen table, Ariel sat down, took a sip of milk, and then picked up one of the slices of bread with peanut butter. She took a bite from the right corner and continued to chew. As she swallowed, the chair she was sitting in suddenly slid into the hallway, trapping her.

The chair pulled Ariel all the way to the front door, which was left open. Once it reached the door, the chair spun around three-hundred and sixty degrees three times before coming to a stop. In shock, Ariel ran out of the front door. When she got outside, she was startled to see the man in the garden across the street, saluting. She ran toward Shepperton Field.

As Ariel reached the field, she could see something in the distance near the edge of the woods, just about to enter them. She could make out the figure of her father. However, what she didn't realise was that Dougie believed he was behind Ariel, chasing her in an attempt to stop her from entering the woods. Ariel tried to scream toward her father, but it was too late.

Dougie stared into the hole of the apple, where he could see his daughter on her knees, crying as she realised that her dad had entered the woods. Ariel didn't know what to do. As Dougie watched her cry, he realised that he had never actually needed to enter the woods. The apple shrivelled in the air and turned to dust. Dougie continued to gaze at the area where the apple had disappeared for about a minute before looking in another direction. He shifted his gaze toward the grandfather clock.

Slowly, the door to the grandfather clock opened just enough for a group of nine enchanted clocks to walk out. They circled around Dougie, maintaining an equal distance between themselves and him. Once they had taken up their positions, they remained still, doing very little. Dougie tried to discern what was happening, looking from one clock to another. He wasn't sure if he was supposed to take the initiative or if they were, and as time passed, he remained perplexed. Dougie turned his attention back to the grandfather clock, waiting for answers.

Suddenly, the walls of the room began to collapse and fall to the floor. As they did, the room transformed into a woodland setting. Dougie's vision shifted completely, and all he could see was in black and white. Within the woodland, he noticed something peculiar—a figure resembling a scarecrow with a head shaped like a fort with an eyeglass. Its lower body seemed to be made of bark.

The way it moved was unlike anything made of wood. It moved fluidly, almost like a samurai. Then, it stopped and looked at Dougie, who started to hear Chinese music emanating from the clocks on the floor. Each clock played a different part of the song, but they all played in unison. The walls began to reconstruct themselves around the room, obscuring the creature in the woods from view.

The clocks on the floor began to circle around Dougie, still in harmony with each other. Dougie watched them circle until they transformed into individual beings of time, each the same size as the clocks they had previously been. Once the last clock transformed, they ceased circling but continued to sing.

Dougie focused his gaze on the creature directly in front of him and stared at it for an extended period without speaking. The creature returned his gaze. They maintained this silent exchange until one of the creatures closest to the grandfather clock decided to return to the clock's doorway. One by one, the other creatures followed suit, entering the grandfather clock, leaving the door slightly ajar.

Dougie continued to stare at the partially open door, his mind racing with uncertainty about what would happen next and whether he should follow them. He remained in his chair, deep in thought.

While pondering his next move, Dougie noticed a woman seated in a corner of the room. The chair she occupied was emerald-coloured, the only other colour Dougie could see apart from black and white. This immediately caught Dougie's attention. As he observed her, he noticed that she appeared to be a cancer patient.

The woman looked seriously ill, with swollen feet, legs, and arms. Her hair was whitened, and her neck glands appeared swollen. She wore gloves on her hands, presumably to reduce swelling. In her left hand, she held a plastic cup with small pieces of ice and a straw. With her right hand, she struggled to extract a piece of ice, which took several attempts.

Once the woman finally managed to place a piece of ice in her mouth, she seemed relieved. She crunched the ice with her teeth and glanced at Dougie. He watched as she finished crunching the ice cube, and as it travelled down her throat, a water tap slowly emerged from her neck. Once fully formed, it hung there on the side of her neck.

Dougie stared at the unusual sight, fascinated and mystified, wondering why this was happening to the woman after eating ice. Strangely, the woman appeared unfazed, and the tap did not seem to cause her discomfort. She altered her blinking pattern, holding her blinks for increasingly extended periods.

Dougie got up from his seat and slowly approached the woman, stopping about a metre away. He continued to observe her for an extended time. The woman maintained her extended blinking, and Dougie's focus shifted to the tap hanging from her neck.

Dougie cautiously extended his right hand toward the tap and placed it on the handle. The woman made no move to stop him, and she continued her extended blinking as Dougie turned the tap. Within moments, liquid began to flow out of the tap, moving toward the grandfather clock. Dougie watched as the liquid flowed along the floor, and he followed it as it moved toward the clock. He opened the door wider and stepped inside.

Chapter Seven: Arms, Legs, and Time.

Dougie descended a stone spiral staircase reminiscent of those found in medieval castles. The stairs emitted a soft glow that illuminated his path as he descended. Upon reaching the bottom, he found himself facing a check-in desk. Behind the desk sat a woman with no hair, wearing an eyepatch and an emerald-coloured robe. Her long, curved nose bore bumps and indents.

Dougie halted and observed the woman, who was engrossed in writing in a leather book using an inkwell and feather pen. He studied her and the surroundings from a distance before taking his next steps. As he finally walked toward the woman, he paused at the desk and looked at her.

The woman set aside her pen and inkwell, then wrote "Dougie Wednesday Woodbridge" into the largest book in front of her. She looked up at Dougie and gestured with her head for him to look behind him. After several gestures, Dougie complied and turned to see a set of wooden steps leading to a weathered rowing boat in a canal. This canal, however, was not filled with water but rather with the universe itself.

The canal was a vast expanse of darkness, filled with stars, galaxies, and energy. Dougie gazed at the celestial surroundings, along with the little rowing boat and the steps leading to it. Behind the boat, a small waterfall of stardust emanated from an emerald crystal, forming a current that kept the boat afloat and propelled it forward.

Dougie turned back to the woman, seeking reassurance that this was where he was meant to go. The woman didn't look at him throughout his observation, no matter how long he waited. Eventually, Dougie shifted his gaze back to the boat and the steps.

With caution, he descended the three steps and reached out with his right leg to find steady footing on the boat. Once aboard, the boat swayed briefly but soon stabilised itself. It began to move forward without Dougie needing to row. As he gazed at the space around him, captivated by a jittering star, Dougie's eyes grew heavy, and the next time he opened them, he found himself still on the boat.

The boat had stopped at a platform, and Dougie, still not fully awake, adjusted to his new surroundings. He remained in the boat, observing the platform with a set of four steps leading to a black door. The door had no handle, and no sounds emanated from the other side. Dougie gazed at the door, then at the space around him with curiosity. He could still see galaxies, stars, and emptiness.

Suddenly, something cold touched his right hand. He looked at his hand and found a purple colour on it. He looked around but saw no immediate source for the colour. When he looked up, he saw the same space canal he had observed before. Something cold touched his left ear, but when he turned to look, there was nothing unusual in sight.

Dougie touched his left ear with his left hand, and upon withdrawing it, he saw a gold colour on his index finger and thumb, with the sticky texture of paint. Rubbing his thumb and index finger together, he found that they began to stick to each other. Perplexed, he looked up again, and this time, a gold blot of space paint landed on his head. More droplets followed, falling on both Dougie and the boat, gradually increasing in volume.

Dougie decided it might be best to disembark from the boat using the steps. The droplets didn't follow him; instead, they continued to land on the boat. As he watched, the boat began to change colour.

Dougie noticed that beneath him, the surroundings continued to reveal the vastness of space. He felt something touch his right hand again, but there was no apparent source. When he looked above, he saw only the expanse of space. Something cold touches his left ear once more, but again, there was no visible cause.

Dougie touched his left ear with his left hand, and upon withdrawing it, he saw a purple colour on his index finger and thumb. He rubbed his thumb and index finger together, noticing they were sticking together. As he pondered this, something cold landed on his head—a blot of gold space paint. More droplets followed, accumulating on both Dougie and the boat.

Dougie decided to disembark from the boat using the steps, as the droplets did not follow him. The boat remained under the shower of paint. He turned his attention to the steps, which led to a small building with a dock. The building had an unusual shape, resembling a corner, with a platform connecting the dock to the structure. Four steps led up to a black door.

The droplets did not follow Dougie; instead, they continued to land on the boat. Dougie turned to face the boat and observed it getting recolored. He noticed that beneath the boat, paint droplets were rising to meet it. Dougie then shifted his attention to the door. At first, he merely stared at it, almost lost in the moment, momentarily forgetting what was happening around him. Gradually, Dougie mustered the courage to approach the door.

He didn't immediately attempt to enter. Instead, he thoughtfully contemplated the door for an extended moment, keeping his focus on it.

The door remained motionless, open but without any hint of movement or sound emanating from the other side.

Dougie cautiously walked toward the open doorway. As he extended his right foot toward the door's entrance, the rest of his body was suddenly pulled inside. Once Dougie was no longer on the outside, the door closed shut, transforming into an emerald crystal. The emerald crystal was the same size as the door, and the building surrounding it disintegrated into dust particles, vanishing entirely.

Dougie found himself in a library, standing in a section dedicated to anything related to Emerald Cove. One book particularly caught his attention—'Arms, Legs, and Time.' The book rested on a stand positioned on a shelf. Dougie picked up the book but did not open it. To his surprise, the book opened on its own, and simultaneously, the room transformed into a theatre stage surrounded by seats. Dougie found himself seated in the theatre, with green curtains concealing what lay behind.

Once Dougie settled into his seat, the curtains began to slowly open. As they revealed the stage, a puppet show commenced. It depicted a house with two parents bidding farewell to their son, who was leaving on his bicycle. The young boy rode away, waving to his parents as he began his bike ride.

The boy pedalled his bike until he reached a shop. Upon arriving, he parked his bicycle by a rack and secured it with a chain. He then entered the shop, navigated through the aisles, and headed to the refrigerated section. There, he paused, gazing at the contents before opening the fridge, which held pastries and sandwiches. He selected a sausage roll and grabbed a small carton of apple juice with an attached straw from the cold drinks section.

Carrying these items to the checkout, the boy paid the cashier with a five-pound note. The cashier placed the note in the register and handed the boy his change. The boy pocketed the change, retrieved his items, and unchained his bicycle.

He mounted his bike and pedalled away, the backdrop changing as he ventured into a field with a woodland beyond. The boy, now sitting on the ground next to his bicycle, began eating the sausage roll he had purchased. Beside him, an open carton of apple juice sat upright on the ground. He had already consumed some of it, as the straw protruded from the carton's top.

As the boy was halfway through his snack, something in his peripheral vision caught his attention. The bent straw within his carton began to rotate slowly. After completing a few rotations, the straw's pace quickened significantly until it resembled a helicopter propeller. Once it reached this stage, the entire drinks carton, along with the straw, lifted off the ground, causing the boy to drop his sausage roll.

The carton of juice soared away from the boy, prompting him to get up and follow its path, which led to the edge of the woods. As the boy stood a couple of metres away from the carton, which was now at his eye level, the carton moved further into the woods, and the boy followed until he was completely within the forest.

When the boy emerged from the woods once more, he was no longer a boy but a naked man holding a drinks carton. He walked over to his bicycle and cycled away. The backdrop shifted to the front of his house as the man placed his bike on the driveway and entered his home, still clutching the drinks carton.

Several nights and days passed, and one night, the boy's parents appeared, carrying a wrapped body in thick plastic sheeting. It was secured

with numerous black cable ties at the top and
bottom and a clear wire around the middle. They
walked toward a car, and the scene shifted to
the Emerald Cove beach. There, they placed the
wrapped body on the pebbles and walked away.

The curtains closed on the stage, leaving Dougie
seated there, trying to process what he had
witnessed. Darkness began to engulf the room,
and the background lights flickered until they
burst. From within the lights emerged a new
light, tiny crystal stars that floated toward the
stage. They illuminated the area as the stage's
curtain collapsed and disintegrated.

The book in Dougie's hand closed, turning into
dust. On the stage, two women dressed in
tuxedos and top hats performed an artistic
dance, incorporating horses and a cart, all
without riders. The horses gracefully leaped off
the stage and onto a cobblestone path that
materialised underneath. This path, initially a

narrow strip of carpet, traversed the theatre and led to the exit.

The horses and the cart trotted through the theatre toward the exit. Dougie watched them briefly, then shifted his focus to the cobblestone path. He rose from his seat and began walking toward it. Meanwhile, the women continued their universal dance on the stage.

As the horses and the cart exited the theatre, the doors remained open, revealing a cobblestone road on the other side. This road sloped downward like a picturesque village hill, reminiscent of Shaftesbury, England, with cottages lining the sides of the road. Above Dougie, the sky mirrored the same scenery. The houses were identical, and before Dougie could fully adapt to this new environment, his body seemed to be taken over.

He was propelled forward at an incredible speed without needing to move his legs, as if something were pushing him from behind. Along the way, Dougie experienced fleeting images, racing past horses, houses, and scenes of poverty in the old village. The cobblestone path gradually gave way to flat stones as he entered a tree-lined archway formed by overhanging trees.

In front of him, he spotted the creature he had previously encountered in the cabin in the woods, right as the walls collapsed. This time, the creature appeared to be walking toward Dougie, though the distance remained constant. As Dougie continued along the path, the eyeglass at the centre of the creature detached itself and began flashing a series of images, hovering at eye level in line with Dougie's gaze.

Dougie concentrated on the eyeglass, while everything around him moved at a rapid pace. The creature from which the eyeglass originated disappeared from view. Nevertheless, Dougie was aware that peripheral to his vision, other unfamiliar creatures were standing and observing him. The eyeglass flashed images that were entirely alien to Dougie, and these images transformed into symbols he had never encountered before.

The eyeglass then metamorphosed into a tear in the universe. Although not particularly large, it was slightly larger than the eyeglass had been. Dougie peered through the tear, attempting to discern if it was what he thought it was. As he focused more intently, a golden dagger adorned with jewels suddenly pierced his head. Dougie collapsed backward onto the floor, with a pool of blood forming around his lifeless body. The tear in the universe sealed shut, leaving Dougie dead with the dagger protruding from his forehead.

Chapter Eight: Corner.

In the very spot where Dougie had once lain lifeless on the floor, there now lay an emerald crystal. Out of nowhere, a red leather box with two black leather straps materialised next to this crystal. For an extended period, nothing else occurred except for the presence of the red box and the crystal coexisting in the same space.

Then, the lid of the red box slowly creaked open, and simultaneously, a hand wearing a red glove with no arm attached floated out of the box. The hand reached out and picked up the emerald crystal before retreating back into the box. Moments later, the gloved hand emerged from the box in a different location, hovering down to place the emerald in front of a door. After setting the emerald down, the glove returned to the box, and the lid snapped shut.

The box that had held the glove bore a similar style to the previous one. The surroundings, including the box and the emerald, gave the impression of a room with walls adorned in various cereal packet covers from an otherworldly place. However, the door was not attached to the walls but was centrally located within the room, metres away from any fixed walls. The door itself was hexagonal and emitted various coloured symbols.

A considerable amount of time passed until the vibrations and frequencies in the room began to change. As they did, the box and the crystal on the floor began to shift. An unusual hum followed, starting faintly and gradually increasing in volume until it became unbearable for the human ear. At this point, both the box and the stone levitated simultaneously into the

air, stopping when they were half the height of
the door.

The box began to contract from all sides
individually until each side had compressed. As
the final side of the box dimpled inwards, the
box shrank until it matched the size of the
emerald stone next to it. The emerald stone
began to expand, but before it could undergo any
significant transformation, the box transformed
into an emerald aura and merged with the
emerald stone. This fusion bathed the room in a
bright emerald light, blinding in its brilliance,
and the hum ceased.

As soon as the blinding light vanished, both the
box and the emerald crystal had disappeared. In
their place, Dougie lay naked, facedown on the
floor, unconscious. The hum resumed, and the
vibrations caused Dougie to intermittently lift
off the floor. Various types of cereal began to
emerge from the walls and fell onto the floor.
Upon hitting the floor, the cereal began to

vibrate and move. The door to the room gradually opened, and as this happened, Dougie levitated to the same height as the crystal and the box had previously.

As he reached that height, pieces of cereal bounced off the floor and struck Dougie before rebounding to a new direction. This continued as more cereal pieces rained down from the walls. Dougie's appearance had changed during his time in the room, appearing to have aged ten years. Seven large rings of cereal formed around him as they continued to fall.

When the door had fully opened, Dougie was propelled downward, passing through the floor beneath. As Dougie vanished from sight, the door to the room closed, and the cereal returned to the walls.

Dougie found himself upright but unconscious, seated inside a retro photo booth with its curtain drawn. A continuous emerald flash of light emanated from within the booth as Dougie remained seated. These flashes varied in duration and timing, intermittently illuminating the space around him.

These lights played a role in stirring Dougie from his unconscious state. His eyes opened slowly, resembling those of a person trying to wake from a drugged slumber. However, his vision was limited, and he could only see the opposite side of where he was seated. Briefly, he glimpsed an image similar to the one he had seen while with the Martials: a chair surrounded by clocks. Yet, his heavy eyelids quickly overwhelmed him, and intermittent flashes of light, as if from a camera, flickered in between.

With great effort, Dougie's eyes fluttered open again, revealing new images. This time, he saw himself in a hospital bed in a dementia ward, with the room featuring a bedside table and a lamp whose emerald glow intermittently shone through the lampshade. But just as quickly,

Dougie's vision grew wavy, leading to another set of images. Dougie struggled to keep his eyes open, much like heavy cat flaps on a weak feline.

His vision shifted once more, and he suddenly found himself on his home sofa after falling asleep. This transition appeared to occur within seconds. Shortly after, Dougie saw steam rising in a rotating motion from a coffee cup in Sheriff Steve Hughes' office. Dougie attempted to communicate with Steve, but his lips wouldn't cooperate, resulting in only a series of grunts that earned him a puzzled look from the sheriff.

Dougie's vision remained a chaotic blend of shaking, spinning, and waviness, offering fleeting glimpses of various scenes. Eventually, he found himself back in the retro photo booth, although these moments were brief. A new flash of colour disrupted his vision, and as Dougie's eyes became less heavy, the curtain to the photo booth slid open. Dougie, curious and alert, cast a sidelong glance to discern who or what was behind the curtain.

The end

Dedicated to Tracey Rose Dominy, also known as Tracey Rose Baker, my beloved mum. I miss you every day and I'm so proud of you. I hope you're having a wonderful time at the Angel High Tea Party.

Dedicated to:

Tracey Dominy

Louise Rudkin

George Rudkin

Charlie Rudkin

Alan Rudkin

Rudy Baker

In Loving Memory of:

Tracey Dominy (Mum)

Patricia Ford

Gina Ferguson

Danny Ferguson

Tony Baker

9 781912 948710